. . . it's very, very late
and I should be
sleeping.

Instead,
I'm dreaming about
lighthouse keeping.

My Little Lighthouse

by Alice Palace

Bearpaw Books

My Little
Lighthouse . . .

guides ships where to go,
standing firm on a rock
when icy winds blow.

I climb up the stairway
to get to the top,
winding higher and higher
then I suddenly stop.

Looking out the window,

I see blue waters
sparkling bright.
Dreaming I jump in and swim,
I shut my eyes really tight!

Let's see,
Let's see,
What can I be?

We're brightly colored salmon
shining in the sun,
swimming up the river
getting ready for the run.

We wiggle, flip, and spin
in the rapids' flow,
sliding down the rocks
round and round we go.

Let's see,
Let's see,
What else can I be?

Look up, look up
into the sky,
we're Canada geese
flying so high.

With graceful wings
we sail home,
in perfect formation
flying paths already flown.

**Let's see,
Let's see,
What else can I be?**

We're quiet crusty clams,
our shells are closed up tight.
We open very slowly
to let in a little light.

Lying on the bottom
of Lake Superior's floor,
stormy waters push us
onto the rocky shore.

Let's see,
Let's see,
What else can I be?

We're great gray wolves
howling late at night,
crouching in the shadows
under the bright moonlight.

Our long shaggy fur,
and large watchful eyes
hide us in the woods
in our special disguise.

Let's see,
Let's see,
What else can I be?

We're busy little sandpipers
with long straight legs,
taking short quick steps
guarding fragile spotted eggs.

Walking and peep-lo-ing,
we stay beside the nest,
but when the eggs crack open,
we still don't get to rest.

I'm a sailor on a ship
chugging slowly out to sea,
standing upon the deck
with stars surrounding me.

I visit foreign ports
unloading coal or grain,
then turn the ship around,
and head back home again.

Let's see,
Let's see,
What else can I be?

We're cute, crawly crayfish
scooting all around.
We scamper on the sand
then burrow underground.

Seeing something yummy,
a tasty tadpole treat,
we scurry out to catch it,
and now it's time to eat.

Let's see,
Let's see,
What else can I be?

Sleek, long, and fast,
I'm a kayaker close to shore,
gliding into rocky caves,
taking time to explore.

Enjoying nature's beauty,
I paddle silently along,
then stop and listen to the loon
sing its lonesome song.

Let's see,
Let's see,
What else can I be?

We're playful river otters
rolling on our backs.
We twist, flip, and turn
playing water acrobats.

When we're done swimming,
then it's time to eat.
We catch a wiggly minnow,
and enjoy our
mini treat.

**Let's see,
Let's see,
What else can I be?**

I love old shipwrecks
resting in water so clear.
I'm a diver, diving deep to see them
wearing my scuba gear.

Spending time exploring,
I'm swimming all around.
Surrounded by blue waters,
I hear Superior's sound.

**Let's see,
Let's see,
What else can I be?**

I'm flying with the seagulls
white, black, and gray.
We're squawking and talking,
we love to soar and play.

Gracefully diving,
we catch fish to eat,

**then float on the
water. . .**

. . . and rock
ourselves
to sleep.

Graphic Design and Illustrations Colorized by Carrie Smeby
Creative Collaboration with Mary Anderson
Technical Assistance by Pamela Costello

A Special Thank You To:
In-Fisherman Magazine
The Minnesota Historical Society
The Great Lakes Group
for permission to illustrate their tugboat *Minnesota*

ISBN 0-9709444-1-1
LCCN TXul-039-008

For more information contact:
Bearpaw Books
P. O. Box 243
Emily, MN 56447
www.bearpawbooks.com

Printed in the United States of America